For Erin Murphy and Joy Peskin
—D.S.

For my Grandma Patti
—S.H.

Farrar Straus Giroux Books for Young Readers
An imprint of Macmillan Publishing Group, LLC
120 Broadway, New York, NY 10271

Color separations by Embassy Graphics
Printed in China by RR Donnelley Asia Printing Solutions Ltd., Dongguan City, Guangdong Province
1   3   5   7   9   10   8   6   4   2

mackids.com

Library of Congress Control Number: 2018055417
ISBN 978-0-374-31286-2

A BOOK FOR Escargot

STORY BY Dashka Slater

PICTURES BY Sydney Hanson

FARRAR STRAUS GIROUX · NEW YORK

Bonjour! I see you are reading a book.
I will try not to distract you.
It can be distracting to have a very beautiful
French snail staring at you while you read.

My name is Escargot, and I am on my way
to check out a book at the library.

It will be a French cookbook, filled with
delicious French recipes.
Escargot is going to cook something new!

You should try something new as well.
Have you ever kissed a snail?
Now might be a good time to try it!

While we are traveling to the cookbook section, we can talk.
Tell me, what is *your* favorite book?

Is it *Goldytentacles and the Three Snails*?

Harry Gastropodder and the Chamber of Salads?

Goodnight Snail?

The Very Hungry Snail?

THE VERY HUNGRY SNAIL

Where the Wild Snails Are?

There are so many books to choose from!
Books about dog superheroes and guinea-pig detectives
and flamingo astronauts and halibut firefighters
all having exciting adventures!

But I must tell you something sad about these books.
So sad you might cry.
I am crying just thinking about it.
Will you wipe my eyes for me?
And also my nose?
It's okay to use your sleeve.

Okay, now I will tell you the very sad thing.

Not one of these books is about a daring snail hero who saves the day.

: Dale the Daring, Dashing, Delightful Dog :

Fred the Fantastic, Fearless, Flying Flamingo ((

Hugh the Highly Handsome Hero Halibut

Greg the Gorgeous, Graceful, Gregarious
~ Guinea Pig ~

Sal the slimy, shy, sad snail

All the books about the snail
make a joke about slow snail or shy snail.
I am not laughing at this joke.

You do not look like a laughing-at-snails person.
You look like a clever person who reads
serious books about handsome animals.
You probably know many fancy words.

gallivant – to travel
or wander for
fun

With these fancy words, you could write a sentence *extraordinaire* like "The gallant gastropod gallivants to the rescue!" which is another way of saying "The daring snail hero saves the day!"

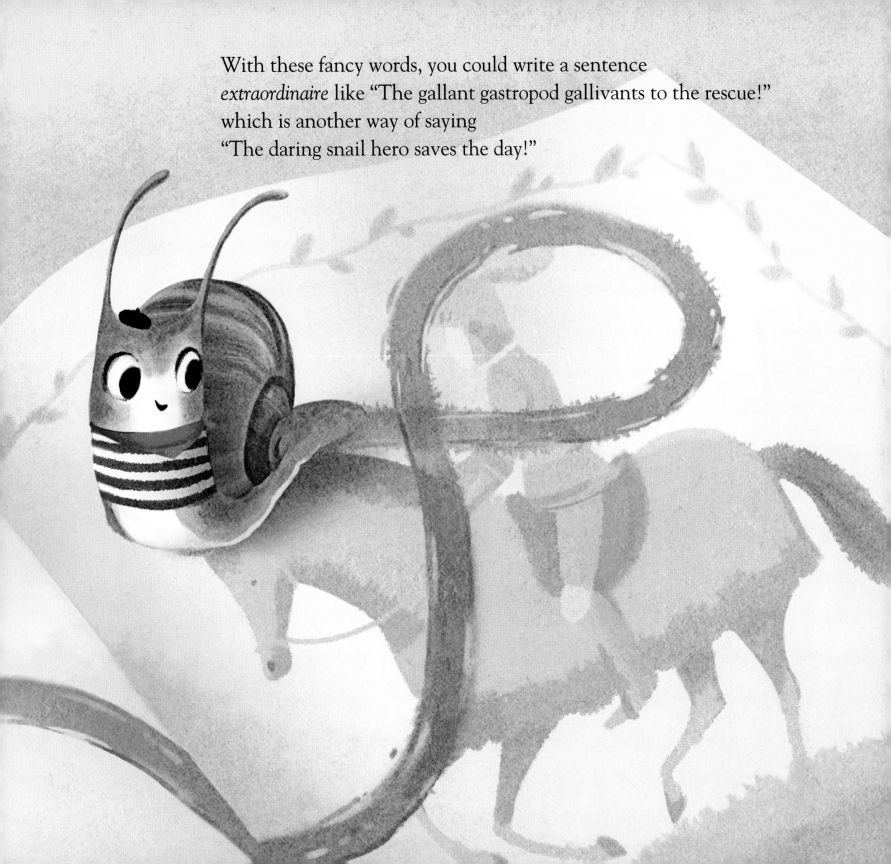

Tell me, have you ever written a book?
You should try it!
Do not worry; Escargot will help you.
It is just like cooking from a recipe.
Add the ingredients, mix them together, and *voilà!*
A perfect story!

Dale the Daring,

Fred the Far

Hugh the Highly

Greg the Go

Sal the slimy, sh

You must begin by introducing the main character.
"Once upon a time, there was a very beautiful French snail hero."
If you want, you can add some details about my most
beautiful parts, like my shiny brown shell or my
translucent tentacles or my *chic* outfit.
Oh là là! You might need to get more paper.

But perhaps you think, "The main character
of a story must have a problem, Escargot!
You are so handsome, suave, and smart.
What problem could you possibly have?"

I will tell you.
Always I eat salad with a few croutons and a light vinaigrette. It is *magnifique*!
But one day I wake up and I have a strange feeling.
I am bored. Bored of eating salad!

and so the gallant gastropod gallivanted off to find a ... recipe for something new to eat.

Maybe I will learn to cook a green bean
or a *soufflé* or a *ratatouille*.
Anything could happen when you have
a daring snail hero like Escargot!

But perhaps you think, "I
cannot wait to find out what
you will cook, Escargot!
Let us get to the cookbook
right away!"

Mais non! It cannot be so easy.
First, the daring French snail hero must overcome an obstacle.
Like this one, for example.

Escargot is very far above the cookbook.
The cookbook is very far below Escargot.
But a daring French snail hero is not afraid of heights.
A daring French snail hero can overcome this obstacle by . . . flying.

You don't believe that Escargot can fly?
Count to three, and I will show you.

One . . .

two . . .

three . . .

That was too fast—I wasn't ready.

Maybe you should count in French:

Un,

deux,

trois!

Still too fast!
I think maybe I need a little push.

Did you see me fly? I was like an eagle!
I just had a little trouble with the landing.

But that does not matter, because I have arrived
at the cookbook!
And now we will have the resolution of the story!

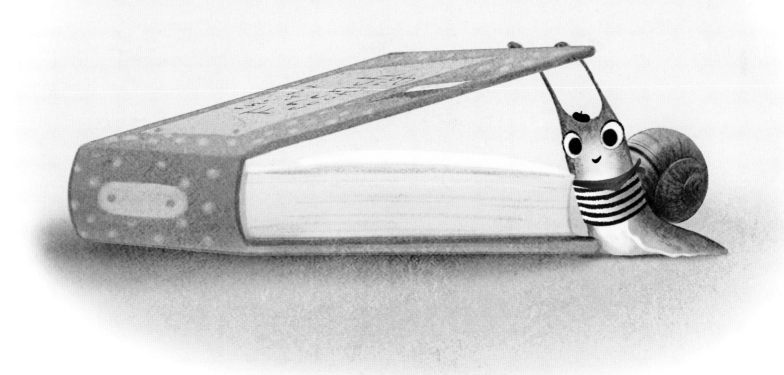

This is the happy part at the end where
the daring French snail hero solves his
problem of being bored with salad by using
the cookbook to make a delicious feast.
Bon appétit!

Escargot

36 snails
4 minced shallots
1 head garlic

2 tbsp butter
2 tsp salt
1 bunch parsley

But this is not the right cookbook.
This cookbook is not about cooking food for Escargot!
This cookbook is about cooking Escargot for food!
The ingredients: garlic, butter, *me*!

What if a French chef comes to the library to check out this book?!
He will cook Escargot for dinner!
You must tell the chef to choose a recipe for French toast

or French bread

or French fries—

but not beautiful French snail!
Also, could you cover me with your hand
so he cannot see me?

While I am inside my shell—
not hiding
but more like
having a private moment—
you can continue writing.

I will start the sentence, and you can finish it.
"Escargot, the daring French snail hero, was not eaten by the French chef because . . ."

Uh-oh.
Escargot might have eaten the cookbook.
I do not think I will be learning how to
cook the green bean
or the *ratatouille* or the *soufflé*.

But . . . on the other hand,
nobody will be learning how to cook *me*!

The daring French snail has defeated the dangerous recipe!
Escargot has saved the day!
This book we have written, it is *magnifique*!

And do you know how it ends?
With a kiss!
Mwah!

THE
END